THESE WORDS

SECOND EDITION

A BOOK OF POEMS BY
STACY HINOJOS

Published by OCYD Publishing

ISBN: 979-8-9912807-1-6

*To my husband and best
friend, Scott.*

*To my sons,
Henry and Joseph
&
Miles and Evan*

A Note from the Author

Thank you so much for purchasing this copy of These Words. I cannot fully express how much I appreciate you taking a chance on a completely unknown author from Central Wisconsin.

You will quickly learn that I like to write in my own style. I've never been one for following the rules concerning self-expression. Personally, I find it too restrictive. The poems remain untitled, mostly due to their short nature, however I find that by placing a title on them, it forces you to interpret the meaning of the words within, instead of finding your own experiences within the words you are holding.

These Words is a collection of mini-therapy sessions that allowed me the opportunity to reflect and heal over the decades. Healing is never a quick journey, but I'm glad that I've found a healthy way of dealing with some of the heaviness. I am sharing these with you, in the hope that you don't feel alone.

With everlasting gratitude,
Stacy

August 31, 2025
Second Edition

I dug this grave,
with my bare hands...

Each handful of earth,
bearing my pain...

Clawing through my anger,
tears washing my face...

I climb into the hole,
body aching with sweat...

Inhaling the mud as I sink,
deeper into nothingness...

To sleep.

Writing the words I long to say,
twisting them as I go.

I don't worry if it doesn't make sense,
alternating rhythms and alternating rhymes.

This is cheaper than therapy,
just letting the words flow.

The madness, anger, and love,
the truth that was lost.

Breathe in and words tumble over each other,
rushing to fall on the page.

I'm done being your apologist

Tired of holding my tongue

No more swallowing my words

And letting the hurt go on

Guarded organ of longing and lust,
Kept locked with an antique key.

Hoping that someone wakes it,
From a deep and lonesome sleep.

The weight of my words,
fall on his shoulders.

They stab his heart,
repeatedly.

I know my will better than he,
I will not let him win.

The disappointment settles in,
as I lay down my head,
knowing this is where I would end.

A pile where all the others are.

The abused.
The disused.
The victims of your tongue.

The lies that have been poured,
poisoning us all.

go ahead

strip down to your soul

get comfortable with your incompleteness

enjoy the breeze

on your bare bones

breathe in all the possibilities

this world can offer you

so much more

now exhale the things that no longer serve

What should you do,
when even happy feels heavy?

When the sunny skies above,
come across dull and grey.

And bird song sounds like
a roaring plane.

Many see darkness and feel dread,
hopelessness, fear.

I choose to embrace it,
to study what lies within.

Search out the answers,
meditate on the pain.

Accept the burden of the extra weight
that lies within my chest.

In the obscurity you find the
truth you buried...

instead of letting it breathe.

The older we become, the more we learn.

We acquire an insight into ourselves,
and of our place on Earth.

We obtain an immense knowledge of not only the beautiful,
but the ugliness that surrounds us.

We receive trust and love,
while gaining wisdom and holding onto hope.

The list continues to grow with each passing moment,
but some of these lessons are not easy to endure.

As the years pass and the seasons change,
we start losing those we love and hold dear.

None of these losses are painless,
no matter how many times we've traveled down this path.

The agony leaving us raw, tearing at our hearts.
Nothing can calm these storms.

No amount of perspective and meditation,
acceptance or prayer,
can bring instant relief to the grief that takes over our lives.

Even in times when death is welcomed,
it bites into us baring its teeth, not willing to let go.

As the clouds roll by,
they change with every move.

Coming, going with the wind,
breezing above the pines and hills.

Coming, going as they please,
just like many of our dreams.

Once upon a time,
I loved deeply,
much too deeply.
I could never appease his need
for love and closeness.
It seemed the more I gave,
the more he craved.
He wrapped a string around my heart,
left me dangle in mid-air.

Draining my soul of
everything I needed to survive,
my heart started to dry.
Like a wilted rose,
I shattered into a million pieces.
I watched him blow the
fragments away in one breath.
And yet
I loved him.

breathe life into these

words of mine

these words you hold

in your hand

syllables that flowed from

a cheap blue pen

onto an old grocery list

I have longed to tell you,
how your words have lingered
in my ears.

On cold nights that
bring bitter winds,
your words come biting back.

Bearing down on me,
stinging and cruel,
glazed with sparkly diamond ice.

Alone in a crowded room,
where no one knows your face.

Fully aware you don't belong here,
and you don't see an escape.

he glances

my way

and suddenly

i am nothing

You fill your days planning what is to come next,
the various outcomes depending on
which game piece you move.

Your head contains detailed notes,
which lie you laid at each person's feet,
what story line needs to be changed.

The best way to control the narrative
that best suits your needs,
and which heart strings need to be pulled today.

I never want to find myself in the position
of barely hanging on ever again...

Especially when someone you love
is standing above you...

Glaring down at you in pity
ready to push because they can...

stolen moments vaporize

wishes and dreams grow cold

love dying more each day

until we both let go

It's difficult to know
who you are.

One moment you are glorious,
like a sun warmed peach.

The next,
the worm inside.

To look in a mirror,
and really look at yourself,
takes courage.

To search beyond the physical scars,
towards the emotional,
shows how fearless you can be.

When once she bloomed,
under the luminous full moon,
she realized that she had been reborn.

Born into the season of snow,
the days ruled short by the sun.
And it was here that she was the happiest.

White around her feet,
cold crisp nights,
and peace in the sky.

Escaping into empty journals,
pen in hand,
opening those hidden wounds,
in an effort to fully heal.

Searching the soul,
self-reflection in the words,
not knowing where your journey ends,
or if you've truly begun.

I've watched you lie.

I've heard them roll off your
tongue like honey.

You never thought I noticed,
but I counted every single one.

which of my paralyzing thoughts

will take my brain hostage tonight

as I lay myself gently off to sleep

what we have

what we hold

deep inside

within our hearts

is Home

Your red flags
are waving red flags.

And you stand there,
laughing at the world.

The world you
set on fire.

Why is life so complicated?
You perceive yourself travelling in circles,
equating simple functions as climbing mountains.

It hurts when you breathe.
You feel tired, worn down, walked on, abused.
No one understands where you feel you are in the world.

You envision your life as a never-ending tangle of yarn,
which you have to unravel alone,
in a darkened room with little light.

And you wonder to yourself,
"Does this have any meaning at all?"

You lose your grip on reality
as it slowly slips between your fingers,
into a void that you didn't see on the horizon.

Is this some person's cruel, sick trick?
Are you a puppet, dangling on one frayed string?

I went for a walk the other day,
and I was thinking of you.

My heart ached.

I looked upwards to the sky for answers,
alas, none came

My heart ached.

I wished for some sort of sign,
the wind gently brushed my cheek.

My heart ached.

The wind whispered in my ear,
I heard you say my name.

My heart ached.

When playing the victim gets you nowhere,
When you find yourself all alone,
Make sure to latch every window,
And bolt all the doors.

Then...
set light to all the rooms.

I wish I could take away the fear,
that reappears to haunt your dreams.

I wish I could ease your pain,
so you don't have to cry in the rain.

I wish I could wash the mud off those memories,
and make them shine like new.

I know I can't,
but I wish I could.

waiting patiently

on a dusty shelf

longing for someone

all alone

to open the cover

and read the words

that long to be read

If you do not understand me,
despite my calm clear words,
then you are putting forth a concentrated effort
into not wanting to know the truth of my utterances.

You refuse to look deeply into the intense
coolness of the well that stands before you,
because you fear what will be reflected back.

Each morning waking,
is an opportunity to embrace
the world in front of you.

The choices you've made,
the choices yet to make.

The blissful moments,
the cruel.

The words you left unsaid,
the words you shouted into the storm.

In this moment,
as you open your eyes,
you will breathe in deeply,
and breathe out "yes" or "no".

sitting on a park bench
no where to go
but home

i don't want to be home
i want to be anywhere
but home

Her soul contains
fire and spite.

Not sugar and spice.

I had that dream again,
the one where I was
engulfed by the
voices in my head.

They tried to
drown me in a tub
of despair.

The more I screamed,
the quieter I became.

Broken.

Battered.

Bruised.

What good is a heart,
if it never gets used?

these words are my therapy

they are my joys and my tears
my nightmares and dreams
hard fought battles and heartache

they are the things that keep me awake at night
and the things that sing me to sleep

these words are my everything

When someone becomes "nothing" to you,
allow yourself to grieve.
Clear the air around you,
of fallen hopes and dreams.

Give yourself permission,
to heal in your own way.
But don't close off the world around you,
you still need to live each day.

Sometimes I wonder about the
stars in their heavenly skies...

The view they must have...

Perhaps they look down and see
our eyes twinkling up at them.

My pen glides silently across the paper.
It is not controlled by my hand or mind alone,
but by my words.

This is my peace of mind.
it is my solace.

It is my silent way of
saying what's on my mind.

No one hears me,
but my pen and paper,
and both are silent critics.

Enemies of the world unite!
For I am sure there are a few,
who dislike my very being,
my existence alone unnerves.

Shout at me all you want!
Use my name in vain!
Punish me with twists and lies,
I'll love you all the same.

you grapple with the happy times

you panic in the calm

actively you choose chaos

even in a storm

Bitterness tore through her
He would quickly learn
That you never cross a woman
Especially her

She would gladly admit her wrongs
Swallow every single lie
Except the ones she told herself
Those kept her alive

He will come to regret
The lessons he never learned
And pray to his heaven
That he was just misunderstood

She lit each match,
to burn every bridge.

Sunk all the life rafts,
then yelled into the wind...

"Why won't someone save me?"

We hold onto things that no longer matter,
allowing them to control our journey,
filling our brains with lies.

Do we do this because we are
attached to a moment,
or have we simply become comfortable with the pain?

The wind travelled a thousand miles,
merely to whisper your name.

And in response,
I blew a kiss your way.

A single touch from her
began healing your old wounds.

Her kisses melted you
into arms soft and warm.

You realized life was worth something,
and you chose to live again.

Winter sets into bones,
like frost upon the windows.

Northern gales steal away breath,
while lashes strain to blink.

Frozen toes and noses,
and crimson flushed faces.

Endless drifts and footprints.
The wind picks up again.

Acknowledgements

This book would not have been possible without the love, patience, and support of my husband, Scott. He was my main editor on this project and helped with the layout. He truly believed that I could accomplish this lifelong dream of mine.

Special thanks to Kelli Cornelius for taking the time to read the manuscript multiple times, and for sharing her sage wisdom.

I am also grateful to a certain Spirit who guided me and gave me a swift kick in the pants when I needed it most.

Yes, this is MY time!

About the Author

Stacy grew up along the shores of Lake Superior, in the Chequamegon Bay area, surrounded by writers, musicians, and artists. She started writing from a young age and continues to write daily, mostly to quiet her mind.

She currently resides in Central Wisconsin with her husband Scott, and their son Henry, but her heart will always call the great north home.

For more information:
https://linktr.ee/SLHinojos

Other Books Available:
A Thousand Melodies
Everything but a Novel